THE JENNY COLLECTION

SERIES TWO

A SUBURBAN HOTWIFE'S ADVENTURES

CHRISTIAN PRICE

CHRISTIANPRICEWRITES.COM

CONTENTS

JENNY AND THE CHASTITY KEY PARTY

SHARED BY FOUR STUNNING WOMEN

"I DON'T THINK THIS IS GOING TO WORK, love," Todd said with a hint of sarcasm in his voice.

Jenny sighed, sitting up on the bed without relaxing her grip around his definitely not-flaccid cock. She could feel him pulsing in her hand, growing harder and harder as each new heartbeat brought more blood, more lust, more desire.

The polished metal chastity cage laid on the sheets next to them. There was no way it was going on just yet.

"Well," she teased with a smile, "I guess we'll have to work together then..."

With that, she began slowly stroking up and down, up and down.

Todd leaned back, grinning at her as he took in the sight of her incredible breasts softly bouncing with each stroke.

She was enjoying herself, teasing every inch of his erection as his hips moved involuntarily against her hand, searching desperately for some relief from the intense pressure that was no doubt building inside of him.

Once he was nice and worked up, she dropped to her knees between his legs and seductively licked the length of his shaft. Her smooth lips wrapped around the head of his cock, and she began taking him in.

"Oh God, Jenny... Fuck..." he moaned, squirming helplessly on the bed as his once sweet, innocent suburban wife slowly took his ample cock in inch by inch.

"Mmmm," she moaned in reply.

"Fuck, you're so good," he groaned, squeezing her nipples in his finger- tips. "I don't know how I got so lucky."

She giggled, just barely avoiding gag- ging over the width of his member while teasing his balls with the tip of her tongue.

Jenny loved giving oral now, and she wondered how things would have been if they had never crossed paths with the sexy lesbian next door.

Vanessa had transformed their sex life, and there was no going back to once-a-week missionary now. Not that she would ever want to!

She watched Todd as he moaned and squirmed with her every move, her lover's eyes rolling back as she brought him to the brink of an orgasm only to slow things down and tease him some more. There was something about feeling such immense power over another that turned her on more than anything else.

Her pussy ached, but she didn't want to give him the pleasure of fucking her. Not just yet. That would have to wait until after she and Vanessa got back from their ladies' night!

But first she had to get Todd's throbbing cock locked up into the tiny steel cage now pressing against her knee. Game on!

She pushed back down, forcing herself to take all of him until his pulsing head was pushing up against the back of her throat.

"Oh Fuck!" he gasped. "FUCK!"

She could feel it coming, his cock tensing up inside of her mouth before unloading a thick stream of hot cum into her throat.

He writhed about on the bed, his fingertips passionately running through her dark brown hair as she swallowed spurt after spurt of his seed.

As her lips slid off of his spent cock, she licked them with her tongue. Not a drop. She was really getting good at this!

"I love you, baby," Todd sighed in total post-orgasm bliss.

Jenny straddled his chest, dipping down to kiss him for a long, sweet moment.

Then it was time to get to work.

She dropped back down to his quickly shrinking cock and easily slid the metal ring over his package. With a little more effort, she securely locked his member up for the night with the only key to his sexual freedom now dangling between her breasts on a silver chain.

"Good boy," she teased. "Now don't you be naughty, because I gonna want everything you've got when I get back tonight!"

That seemed to send Todd's imagination reeling, his cock pulsing against its cage.

He was at her mercy now; they both knew it.

———

"WELCOME! YOU MUST BE JENNY?"

She stood there for a long moment, Vanessa by her side, as she unconsciously ogled the incredible woman before her. Bleach blonde hair fell on her shoulders, leaving nothing to the imagination. The woman wore nothing at all, in fact, save for the silver necklace and key hanging between her breasts.

"Uh... yeah!" Jenny said, snapping out of her trance.

The woman just smirked at her with at least a hint of seduction in her eyes.

"And Vanessa! I'm glad you could make it."

"Same, you look stunning as ever, Chastity!" Vanessa replied, making no effort to hide her own interest in their host for the evening.

"Please, come in."

They stepped inside to a beautiful private courtyard within, filled with exotic plants perfectly accentuated by tasteful lighting design.

In the center was a large fire pit, illuminating the silhouettes of two figures sitting close together, very close together, facing the fire.

"Wow," Jenny marveled, "this is so beautiful!"

"Thank you," Chastity replied before gesturing to a door. "The restroom is right here, so you can get changed. Don't take too long in there, ladies!"

"I'll try not to keep her tied up too long," Vanessa purred, her very words making Jenny wet with anticipation.

No words were spoken.

The moment the bathroom door was closed and locked, the two women were wrapped in each other's embrace.

Vanessa's tongue probed Jenny's soft lips as their hands roamed over each other's bodies, stripping off layers of clothing, until Jenny stopped for a moment at the unfamiliar touch of cold metal.

"What..." she hesitated.

Taking a step back, Vanessa did a twirl to show off the polished metal chastity belt locked securely around her waist, preventing any potential access to her pussy. And Jenny sure loved that pussy!

"That's not fair!" she said, feeling suddenly vulnerable in her nakedness.

Perhaps she could get the key, hanging around Vanessa's neck, with a little more persuasion.

"Oh, really?" Vanessa shot back. "And why is that?"

"Because... Oh fuck..."

Jenny didn't have time to finish her thought before Vanessa had pushed her back against the bathroom counter, spread her legs, and dropped to her knees to attend to her slick lips.

She moaned as Vanessa's tongue softly traced her slit before circling her clit and going in for the kill.

"Oh, God!" Jenny gasped.

"Yes?" Vanessa teased before returning to the task at hand.

In less than thirty seconds, Vanessa had her body quivering as a powerful orgasm rippled through her body, sending waves of pleasure crashing in every direction.

Just then, Vanessa's fingers found their way into her pussy, pressing tight against her g-spot and forcing another orgasm out just after the first.

"Oh Fuck! Fuck! FUCK!"

Jenny was moaning uncontrollably, her cries of pleasure no doubt loud enough to be heard outside the small bathroom.

KNOCK. KNOCK. KNOCK.

The sound came as Vanessa slowly let her down from her high.

"Yes?" Vanessa said, seeing as Jenny was in no position to respond at the moment.

"Vanessa, what did I say?!" Chastity teased from the other side.

"Sorry, not sorry!"

"Hey!" a different woman said from the other side, "you can't keep the new girl all to yourself!"

"Fair enough," Vanessa said.

They opened the bathroom door, standing there like two sluts who'd just been caught in the act. Which was exactly what had happened.

Chastity and two other equally stunning women stood outside, grinning from ear to ear. Each of them had a key hanging from a necklace, and one of them had a chastity belt like Vanessa's.

"I'm Tiffany," said the one who'd just complained about Vanessa not sharing.

"And I'm Jasmine!" said the one with the chastity belt.

"Jenny," she said with a touch of embarrassment. "Nice to meet you."

"Oh girl," Jasmine said, "the pleasure will be all ours!"

With that, they turned and led the way towards... somewhere.

Vanessa slapped Jenny's ass, making her giggle. She followed them, wondering what Jasmine might have meant.

Whatever she had in mind, Jenny couldn't wait to find out.

———

THE WARM FLICKER OF THE FIRE CAST A SOFT orange glow on the five naked women gathered around it. They'd spent the better part of an hour sharing stories of sexual adventure — some with their partners, some without.

Jenny sat in awe of these women.

These beautiful women.

These seemingly 'normal' women.

These women she'd never have guessed loved to fuck their friends whenever the opportunity presented itself.

There was no bullshit here, just authenticity. A whole new world was opening before her eyes, and Jenny had never felt so at home.

"So, Jenny, what about you?" asked Tiffany. "What's your story?"

She could see that all eyes were on her now, eyeing her up and down in anticipation.

With a deep breath, she dove into the story of how in the hell she'd ended up here.

How a package accidentally dropped on the wrong doorstep had led to the discovery of a part of her, and of Todd, that she'd never known existed.

How Vanessa had been so very helpful in opening her up, and in more ways than one!

And how that had somehow, against all odds, changed their marriage so completely and so perfectly.

As the words rolled off of her tongue, Jenny could hardly believe that the story she told was her own. But it was!

What is this life?

By the time she'd finished her story, the four women had moved in close around her. Their soft, smooth bodies touching her, their fingertips caressing her, their lips kissing her.

"Oooh!" Jenny cooed as someone, she didn't care who, began touching her pussy.

She was more wet than she'd imagined, and the sudden realization sent her heart racing.

"Wait! Wait! Wait!" Chastity interrupted. "Not just yet. You all know the rules!"

Jenny looked up at the sensual figure standing above her, silhouetted by the flicker of the firelight.

She slowly removed her key necklace, dropping it into a glass bowl with a soft clink.

One by one, the other girls dropped their necklaces and keys into the bowl as well.

Finally, Chastity presented the bowl to Jenny.

"Each of us puts in a key," she explained, "and at the end of the night, we each get a key back."

"If you get lucky, you might pick your own," Tiffany said.

"But if you get really lucky," Vanessa teased, "you might pick someone else's."

Jenny looked at each of them.

They were serious.

"And how do I know who has mine?" she asked timidly.

"You don't, girl!" Jasmine laughed. "You'll have to sleep around and find out!"

The girls giggled at that, and Jenny's heart skipped a beat.

Her hands reached up, unclasping her chain.

She wasn't sure how Todd would react to this, but she was willing to take that risk.

With a metallic clink, the key to her husband's pleasure landed in the bowl with the others.

"Now girls," Vanessa purred, "let's play!"

Four sexy women pounced onto Jenny like hunters going in for the kill, and she was their willing prey.

Her back arched, and a moan escaped her lips as Chastity dropped to her knees and began licking her pussy while Tiffany and Jasmine went to work on her breasts.

Vanessa, flexible as ever, got herself right in the middle. Kissing and nipping at her neck before working her way up to her lips for a long, sensual kiss.

"Fuck, I'm gonna..." Jenny gasped.

"Yes!" Vanessa whispered, looking Jenny deep in the eyes. "We want you to cum."

"Mmmmm...Fuck!"

She shook, gasping for air as the first of many orgasms washed over her.

The other three continued playing with her body, teasing and pleasuring every inch while Jasmine quietly retreated just long enough to slip on a strap-on dildo.

"Come here, you," she instructed.

Jenny complied, moving onto her knees on the couch with the others' help.

"Oh, fuck!" she gasped as the head of the silicon cock pushed deep into her.

It was big. Enormous actually. Just how she liked it!

"You like that, girl?" Jasmine asked.

"Um... yes!" she got out between her gasps of pleasure.

Someone giggled in response, and Jenny was suddenly at ease with the whole situation.

She arched her back more, pushing her ass up towards Jasmine so she could fuck her even harder.

Vanessa slipped a hand below and found her clit, stroking it between two fingers while Jasmine continued to pound her from behind. The sensation sent shivers racing through Jenny's body.

She could feel herself getting ready. And with one more flick from Vanessa's fingers, Jenny came.

This time, she came hard. And the waves of pleasure didn't stop, they just kept crashing over her body again and again and again.

When she was finally done, all four women gathered around her.

Touching, caressing, licking, and fucking with their hands, tongues, dildos and fingertips, until they'd gotten each other off too.

All except Jasmine and Vanessa, that is, who'd been denied their own pleasure for the evening.

It was the most beautiful, erotic thing Jenny had ever seen. And she had a front-row seat to the whole thing!

————

BEFORE LONG, IT WAS TIME TO WRAP UP and head home for the night.

Chastity held out the bowl as each woman blindly reached in to grab a key.

They reluctantly dressed, shared phone numbers, and kissed each other goodbye.

When they pulled into the driveway, they could see Todd had left the porch light on. He was no doubt anticipating their return, eagerly waiting for his turn with Jenny's now well-fucked pussy.

She was pretty sure she'd picked out the same key she'd put in, but there was only one way to find out!

"You've got this, Jen," Vanessa encouraged, planting a soft kiss on her lips before heading their separate ways.

With a deep breath, Jenny opened the door and stepped inside.

The house was quiet, but a light coming from their bedroom told her Todd must be waiting there. She silently crept up the stairs, hoping to surprise him.

But when she got to the bedroom, there was no sign of Todd.

"Hello, love!" he whispered in her ear, making her jump in surprise.

His arms wrapped around her waist, hugging her from behind and pressing his steel cage against her ass through the thin fabric of her dress.

He might have been caged, but he was certainly hard!

"How was your evening?" he asked.

She turned around, smiling up at this man who somehow not only approved of her doing all this, but seemed to love her all the more for it!

"It was something else."

"Not your typical girls' night out?"

"Not exactly," she giggled. "I'm not sure your typical girls' night out includes cumming your fucking brains out more times than any of us could count!"

A fire of desire sparked in his eyes at that.

"Fuck, you're so sexy!"

His lips met hers in a passionate kiss. The kind of kiss not even Vanessa with her soft lips and smooth ways could rival.

Soon he was helping her out of her dress, caressing her body, and gently probing her slit with his firm fingertips.

"I think you should unlock me now," he whispered in her ear.

This was it!

Jenny took a deep breath. She unclasped the chain, inserting the key into the lock on his stainless steel cage.

Or at least attempting to.

"Shit!" she said with a hint of sarcasm in your voice.

"What is it?" Todd asked, though she suspected he knew the answer.

"I must have switched keys with someone else," she explained. "It was a key party, after all!"

Todd sat back, studying her face and realizing she wasn't joking.

"Well then," he said slowly, "I guess we'll have to figure out who has that key."

"I guess so..."

A smirk crossed his lips, and he looked as if he was about ready to devour her.

"My, my, love," he teased. "So naughty!"

"You know it!" Jenny laughed, moving towards the edge of the bed.

It was late, and she was damn tired from all the earlier action!

But Todd's arms wrapped around her waist again, pulling her back onto the bed below him.

He straddled her body, just like she'd done earlier that night, kissing her lips before pulling back to take it all in.

"You're so beautiful," he whispered, seeming to lose his focus for a moment. "But don't think for a moment you're going to get off that easy!"

With an almost sadistic smile, he dropped between her legs.

His tongue ran up and down her slick slit. How she was still turned on after everything that had happened was beyond her. Yet, here they were.

"Okay, lover boy," Jenny purred, "do your worst..."

Todd smiled and got right to work.

The tip of his tongue pushed past her outer lips and slid up and down the length of her wetness, making her moan as his tongue flicked her clit and teased the sensitive flesh.

"Oh, fuck..." she moaned, biting her lip as the pleasure rose within her.

Her hips moved up and down as if she was riding him instead of the other way around.

His tongue continued to lick and tease while his hands moved up and grabbed both breasts, kneading them and pinching her nipples as he continued his assault on her pussy.

The room spun as her orgasm approached and she came again, crying out Todd's name as her pussy spasmed around his tongue.

"That feels so good, baby... Oh fuck..." she cried out. "YES!"

JENNY AND THE FIRST-TIME SWINGERS

THEIR FIRST FOURSOME WITH FRIENDS

"So, now what do we do?" Todd asked, having just finished giving her yet another orgasm.

She'd long since lost track of how many she'd had in the last few hours. As if her ladies' night escapades hadn't been enough, her devoted husband had kept 'em coming — to keep her cumming — ever since she'd come home.

But his question snapped her back into reality.

"Um... I don't know."

Her husband's cock was trapped in its stainless steel cage, and without the key he wouldn't be cumming soon.

How was she supposed to get that key back?

Jenny didn't know.

"Maybe you should call Vanessa?" he hinted.

"Oh! Good idea."

She crawled to the edge of their bed, her bare body glistening with the sheen of her own cum now trickling down her thighs.

Her legs trembled as she stood up, the aftershocks of countless orgasms still reverberating through her as she fumbled through her purse to find her phone.

RING. RING.

"Hello, slut!" Vanessa answered.

"Hey, Vanessa."

There was no sense in denying her label. She'd earned it tonight. Jenny had been quite the naughty little slut. And she was okay with that.

"What can I do you for?"

She should have known damn well what! It had been Vanessa, their stunning next-door neighbor, who'd invited Jenny to the key party.

"We're looking for a key," Jenny answered.

"I see. I'll be right over!"

Despite her best efforts, Vanessa's voice betrayed the fact that she was more than a little excited about this turn of events.

———

SURE ENOUGH, SHE WAS STANDING ON THEIR doorstep not one minute later!

"Come in," Todd said.

He'd gone down to answer the door since Jenny was in no state to do so at the moment. She heard the familiar click of Vanessa's heels as she followed Todd up the stairs to the bedroom.

"Long time no see!" she smirked while strutting into their bedroom as if she owned the place.

For the moment, Jenny supposed, she may as well have.

"Oh, I suppose you're looking for this?" Vanessa teased, already knowing the answer.

She bent down seductively, showing off the silver key dangling between her perky breasts.

"You know it!" Jenny replied.

"And what about you, Todd?" she asked, eagerly dropping to her knees before Jenny's husband and undoing his fly. "Oh, my! What do we have here?"

Vanessa might have been a lesbian, but she sure seemed to enjoy playing around with a cock now and then. Especially a caged one!

"Mmmm," Todd cooed, trying his best not to lose his head while Vanessa lightly stroked his exposed balls with her fingertips.

"Jenny," Vanessa said, "why don't you come and help me with this?"

She was really playing it up tonight, but Jenny went along for the ride.

Taking her place beside Vanessa on the floor, she reached for the key only to find her lips met with another's.

For at least the second time that night, they were making out. And this time, Jenny's husband was watching.

The thought sent a tingle through her pussy.

They broke away from each other for a moment when Jenny finally got the key free.

"Moment of truth!" Vanessa teased.

Jenny inserted the key into the lock and...

Nothing. It didn't budge.

"Fuck!" Jenny cursed.

Vanessa laughed, standing back up and returning the worthless key to her neck. With her heels on, she towered above both of them.

"Well, that sucks for you!" she whispered in Todd's ear, loud enough for both of them to hear.

"What do we do?" Jenny asked, her fingers still holding her husband's cold metal cage.

"It's simple. You just get together with the other ladies, one by one, until you find a match!"

"Vanessa, what the fuck?" Jenny said, standing up to her.

"Jenn, it's okay..." Todd reassured.

"No, it's not okay!"

"Listen, Jenny," Vanessa said in the least sarcastic tone she'd conjured yet. "You'll get the key back. And you will thank me later. Just trust me."

Before she could respond, Vanessa had waltzed out of the room and was on her way out the front door.

"Best of luck to you both!"

Just like that, she was gone. Jenny stood naked before her husband, searching his expressions. Hoping she hadn't gone too far this time, let her guard down too much.

"Sounds like you've got some calls to make, love," he smiled.

They were good.

————

JENNY AND TODD WAITED OUTSIDE THE door as the sound of hurried footsteps approached from inside. With the deep click of a deadbolt unlocking, the door opened to reveal a slightly flustered blonde bombshell on the other side.

"Jenny!" she squealed in delight.

"Tiffany, good to see you again! This is my husband, Todd."

"Nice to meet you."

"Come on in," Tiffany invited. "Nathan's just finishing up in the kitchen."

She ushered them into the living room, where they sat down together on a couch opposite two chairs. Tiffany sat in one, while her husband emerged from the kitchen a moment later.

"Charcuterie, anyone?" Nathan asked.

"Please!" Jenny smiled, thankful that the slightly awkward silence in the room had broken.

Nathan set the tray down on the coffee table and took a seat next to his wife.

"Thank you," Todd said as he picked out a cracker and a cheese slice to go with it.

"So, um..." Jenny began.

"Oh, sorry!" Tiffany said, procuring the key around her own neck from under her blouse. "We're new to this!"

"Same," Todd laughed.

"How did you two get into the lifestyle?" asked Nathan.

Jenny and Todd looked at each other for a second, unsure of what he meant.

"What is the lifestyle?"

Tiffany giggled in response.

"Don't worry. That's a good question!" she began. "The lifestyle. Ethical non-monogamy. Swinging. All different terms describing the same thing..."

"...fucking with friends!" Nathan quipped.

Todd laughed, and soon the four of them were deep into discussing the incredible journeys that had led each of them to this point — to sitting on a couch in a stranger's living room with the very real possibility that they'd soon be stripping each other's clothes off and, well... fucking with friends.

What is this life?

As they'd candidly admitted, Tiffany and Nathan were relatively new to this as well. They'd had a MFM threesome with a single guy, but had never 'played' with another couple before. So they were in the same boat, roughly.

Jenny was more than a little intrigued by the thought of two hard cocks taking her at the same time. That was something she'd have to think long and hard about later.

But for now, there was the more pressing matter of getting back the key to her husband's freedom.

"So..." Jenny finally asked, holding up her own key. "How do we do this thing?"

"Well," Nathan began, "we could just swap keys and see what happens."

"Or," Tiffany interrupted, "we could get out of these clothes first..."

There was a second's hesitation as the four individuals seemed to run through the possibilities in their minds.

"I like the second option," Todd smiled, unbuttoning his shirt as Nathan did the same.

Tiffany stood up and pulled her sundress down over her shoulders. It fell to the floor without a sound as the room stood still for a moment.

She wasn't wearing anything underneath. And she was absolutely stunning.

The boys resumed their disrobing, while Tiffany made her way over to the couch and started helping Jenny out of her own clothes.

Nathan, now naked except for his own black plastic cage, nestled in behind his wife as Todd did the same.

They were all so turned on by each other's bodies right then that Jenny struggled to keep her hands off of them.

Tiffany was a good kisser, too.

She was soft and gentle, totally different from Todd or Vanessa.

Jenny couldn't get enough of her!

Her hands wandered across Tiffany's body as Todd joined in.

"Is this okay?" he asked her.

"Absolutely," Tiffany reassured.

With a seductive smile in his direction, Nathan joined in the fun as well, running his fingertips up and down Jenny's side before coming up to knead her breasts.

Their bodies seemed to melt together on that couch as if four individuals had suddenly, by some indescribable wonder, become one.

They kissed.

They touched.

They fondled.

Jenny's fingers worked their way down to Tiffany's slit, both of them gasping as they simultaneously discovered just how turned on she was.

"You're soaking wet!" Jenny whispered, wrapping her other hand around Tiffany's neck as their lips met in a fiery kiss.

With a little help from their enthusiastic husbands, Jenny was soon in position straddling Tiffany, making out as their bodies sensually pressed against each other's.

Jenny's fingers pushed their way into Tiffany's pussy, and she moaned in response.

"Yes, yes!" she cooed between kisses.

Tiffany pulled back and kissed her deeply, moaning into Jenny's mouth as her thumb found its way to her clit and she began slowly circling it.

Nathan came up for his own kiss, stealing Tiffany back while Todd did the same with Jenny.

Then, after a beautiful moment making out with their own wives, they suddenly broke off only to find their place again at the lips of the other's partner.

Todd and Tiffany looked so good, so natural together.

And so did Jenny and Nathan.

It all just felt so... so right.

"Mmmmm," Tiffany moaned as a soft orgasm rocked her body. "Yes!"

Jenny was ready to join her, and they both let their bodies slide down the couches as they took turns kissing each other.

Their hands roamed over each other's bodies as they embraced, their tongues meeting in a passionate embrace as her orgasm faded away.

"I want to taste you," Tiffany whispered, sending Jenny's heartbeat racing.

Their husbands must have heard as well, and were once again eager to help with repositioning.

Jenny was quickly sat up on the edge of the couch, her legs spread wide by Todd on one side and Nathan on the other.

Tiffany dropped to her knees on the floor before her, running her hands along Jenny's inner thighs and making her moan with anticipation.

She slowly, seductively ran her tongue up and down her labia, holding out until Jenny was squirming with desire — her body practically begging for the pleasure she was about to receive.

Todd and Nathan instinctively traded off between kissing her and sucking at her nipples, a tantalizing contrast of sensations as Tiffany's tongue suddenly thrust deep into her pussy before retreating to tease her clit.

She went back and forth between the two, bringing Jenny closer and closer to the brink of orgasm.

It didn't take long.

She let out a deep gasp of pleasure as an orgasm rippled through her.

Then another.

And then another.

When her high finally died down, she collapsed back onto the couch.

"That was," Jenny gasped, "so good!"

"You're telling me!" Tiffany teased in response, leaning in for another fervent kiss.

As the girls sat side-by-side catching their breaths, Todd and Nathan patiently waited their turns.

"Um…" Todd finally interrupted after a long moment.

They all laughed at that, the beautiful laugh that's entirely unique to two couples who've just shared the most intimate parts of themselves with each other.

Tiffany took her necklace off while Jenny did the same.

They carefully placed the keys in each other's hands, then turned their attention to their respective husbands.

Jenny wrapped her fingers around her husband's caged cock, feeling him pulse against her as he pressed against it.

He was so ready!

The key, once again, wouldn't turn.

Jenny looked up at her lover, disappointment in her eyes.

"I'm sorry," she mouthed silently.

He just smiled and shook his head. There was no hint of disappointment in his eyes. Only love. Love for her.

"No luck?" Tiffany asked.

Jenny shook her head.

"Us too."

Well, that was a relief, at least. She would have felt terrible had Nathan gotten his freedom and Todd been left wanting.

"Hey," Nathan said, interrupting their gloom. "That just means we get to play with more people, right?"

Todd laughed, giving Nathan a fist bump.

"Men..." Jenny teased.

She stood up, ready to retrieve her things.

But Tiffany and Nathan weren't going anywhere. In fact, she was hard at work licking and sucking her husband's cock through the cage.

"What?" she asked.

Tiffany paused for a moment, looking back and forth between Jenny and Todd with a big smile.

"Oh, please don't tell me you've never seen a man cum in a cage before!"

"Um..." Jenny said shyly.

"Well, with a vibrator. But like... this?" Todd asked, clearly intrigued.

"You're missing out!" Nathan chimed in. "There's nothing quite like having that tight cage wrapped around you while she's... ooohhh."

Tiffany had returned her mouth to her husband's cock, and his words suddenly left him.

"Well, shall we?" Jenny asked Todd, hesitant.

"Please!" he eagerly replied.

Jenny dropped back down to her knees, watching Tiffany and mimicking her actions.

"Oh, fuck..." Todd moaned softly at the sensations.

Jenny licked him slowly at first, letting him adjust to the feeling. Then she began sucking him harder, making him squirm.

She quite liked the control she had over him like this. They'd have to try this at home sometime!

"Ahh... I'm gonna cum..." Nathan gasped next to them.

They watched as Tiffany sat back, using her hand to pull back and forth on Nathan's cage as his cock began pulsing violently. Thick white streams of cum shot out from his cage, coating Tiffany's breasts in his warm seed.

"Mmm... You're so good!" he moaned softly as his orgasm faded.

Tiffany sat up next to him, stroking his hair softly as she wiped the cum from her chest with Nathan's shirt.

Jenny continued her onslaught, but the thick metal cage made it harder for Todd to feel the sensations.

"I don't think it's going to happen, love," he whispered, caressing her cheeks with his fingertips.

"I'm sorry..." Jenny started.

"No, no," Todd interrupted. "Come here."

He gestured to the space beside him, and Jenny joined them.

The two couples laid side by side on the couch, their naked bodies touching each other's as they enjoyed the sensuality of the moment. They cuddled there for a while, then finally got up and reluctantly put their clothes back on.

They said their goodbyes and promised to see each other again soon. With both of their husbands back in action, it was sure to be an ever more wild ride!

———————

ON THE DRIVE HOME, JENNY GOT AHOLD OF Chastity to make plans for that night.

She'd been the host for the key party that had kicked off this whole adventure, and Jenny was excited for Todd to see their incredible home for himself.

And, if she was being honest with herself, she was rather looking forward to the chance of playing with the incredibly attractive Chastity again, too.

The benefits of being a bisexual... swinger? Were they really swingers now?

She looked over at Todd, blissfully smiling as he drove them home from their afternoon fuck session with the friends they'd known for less than 24 hours.

Were they really swingers now?

Jenny figured so. And she liked that very much indeed.

JENNY AND THE HOT TUB HOOKUP

SKINNY DIPPING WITH SWINGERS

Jenny's eyes fluttered open as the glare of the setting sun pierced through the sheer curtains of the bedroom.

Beside her, Todd was still sleeping.

He looked calm, at peace... content. That was the word.

The last few weeks had totally upended their lives, and now things seemed to only be speeding up.

Yet, in the still and quiet moments, Jenny had a sense that things were going to work out just fine for them. That opening up would be the secret sauce that would help them grow and thrive as a couple.

She smiled at the thought, moving closer to him and snuggling her naked body up against his.

And that's when the cold metal cage still locked around his cock brought her back down to earth.

Damn that thing!

She wanted her husband, and she wanted him now.

Jenny would have to wait.

BEEP. BEEP. BEEP.

The alarm clock rang louder and louder.

It was game time.

"Todd, time to wake up," she whispered in his ear.

He moaned something incoherent in response.

"Oh Todd," she said louder.

This time he attempted to roll away from her, but she was too fast for him.

"Time to get up, Todd!" she teased, wrapping her fingers around his cock and giving it a firm squeeze.

That did the trick.

———

KNOCK. KNOCK.

Todd knocked on the heavy door until they heard footsteps approaching from inside.

They'd arrived right on time, as per usual, and were quite possibly over-dressed for the occasion, also as per usual.

"Hello again!" Chastity smiled.

Like last night, she was dressed in absolutely nothing but her necklace. The key dangling from landed at just the right height to draw one's attention to her perky nipples.

And Jenny could see out of the corner of her eye that Todd had noticed.

"Uh..." he stumbled. "Hi, I'm Todd."

He held out his hand, as if introducing himself at a business meeting.

Their gracious host found that quite amusing.

"Chastity!" she laughed, taking his hand and pulling him inside the door. Jenny followed, closing it behind them just as Chastity turned a handshake into a hug followed up by a very friendly kiss on the lips.

Jenny didn't miss out on the action either! Chastity came for her next, holding her tight and kissing her with lips that tasted sweet like... pineapple? Yes, like pineapple.

They walked through the courtyard where the ladies had spent the previous night making friends and making love by the flickering glow of the fire.

But there was no fire tonight.

Instead, Chastity led them around the corner of the house, to a more private area with a table and chairs beside a steaming hot tub.

"Oh, hello there!" a man sitting in the tub said, standing up without a second's thought as his metallic cage shimmered in the lights. "I didn't hear you come in. I'm Mark!"

"Nice to meet you," Todd said, this time awkwardly shaking hands.

"And you must be Jenny?" Mark asked, turning to her.

She nodded.

"I've heard so much about you!"

Jenny blushed, remembering the debauchery that she'd eagerly took part in the night before.

"Oh, it's okay dear!" Chastity encouraged. "You were absolutely lovely last night."

"I feel like a bit of a slut," Jenny confessed sheepishly.

"Oh, no!" Mark protested.

"Jenny, dear..." Chastity said with a sarcastic wink. "We are all sluts here."

She smiled, supposing that was true. After all, Chastity had been intimately involved in the previous night's adventures!

Their hosts motioned towards the chairs, and they took a seat as Mark dried himself off and wrapped a towel around his waist.

Chastity, of course, didn't mind being the only one naked. She seemed to enjoy it, in fact.

"We thought," she said, "since you're both pretty new to this, we could start tonight off with a little game."

"Ooh!" Jenny squealed with delight. "I like games!"

Todd almost rolled his eyes at that. Games were something they'd always agreed to disagree on. She loved them, while he found them excruciatingly boring.

"It's a simple game, really," Chastity explained. "Pick a card from the top of the deck and answer the question or do the action. Just ask for consent first, of course."

"Consent?" Todd questioned.

"I guess that's not something that typically comes up in a card game!" Mark laughed. "I take it you've never played a game quite like this..."

Mark held up the card deck, showing off the sexy illustration on the back of the card — a sexy illustration featuring four sensual bodies entangled in one another's. Pretty much how Jenny imagined an artist might portray what they themselves had done that very morning with their newly christened swinger friends.

"Well, that looks fun," she giggled.

"You've got my attention," Todd said. "And that's saying something for a card game!"

"Shall we?" Chastity asked, motioning to the deck. "I'll go first!"

She reached down and grabbed a card from the top of the pile, her breasts swaying ever so slightly as she did.

"You like that?" she asked, glancing back and forth between Todd and Jenny while deliberately shaking her boobs for them. She was certainly observant!

"I do..." Todd confessed, and Jenny couldn't help but smile.

"We do."

"Once in a generation boobs right there, folks," Mark joked. "Enjoy them while you can!"

Chastity refocused on the task at hand, holding the card up to the light so she could read it.

"How did you get into the lifestyle?" she read. "First off, do y'all know what the lifestyle is?"

"Swingers!" Jenny boldly declared, as if she hadn't just learned the answer to that question earlier that day.

"Very good, dear," Chastity smiled. "Well, Mark and I have been together for about three years, married for two. This is our second marriages, for both of us. When we met, I wasn't looking to jump back into monogamy again. Neither was he. So we started off in the lifestyle from the beginning of our relationship!"

"And look at us now!" Mark said, leaning over to plant a big kiss on his wife's lips. "Okay, my turn now!"

He drew a card, chuckling as he read it silently.

"Lose an article of clothing," Mark said. "That figures."

He stood up slowly and removed his towel with the dramatic flair of a matador teasing a bull.

Except there was no bull. Just Mark's locked up cock they'd all seen five minutes earlier.

"Not quite the effect I was going for," he laughed, taking his seat. "You're up, buddy."

Todd grabbed a card from the top and read it aloud.

"Kiss and nibble on one person's neck or ear until they giggle or moan," he said with a grin. "Well, alright then!"

Todd leaned in to place a soft kiss on Jenny's collar bone, working his way up her neck until he was nibbling on her ear.

His kisses were slow and deliberate, and Jenny wasn't sure whether she should giggle or moan at the sensation.

What came out was a mixture of the two. Her body shivered as he leaned back again, offering her the next card.

She read the card silently, a mischievous smile forming on her lips as she did.

"Lose an article of clothing," she said in a sultry voice.

Jenny pushed her chair back, standing up slowly and seductively as the others watched in anticipation.

"Would you like to help me out of this?" she asked their host.

Chastity eagerly jumped up, giving her a soft kiss on the back of her neck as she carefully unzipped the back of her dress.

"Mmmm," Chastity moaned as Jenny's dress rolled off her shoulders.

Borrowing a page out of Tiffany's book, she'd come dressed in nothing but the cute little dress which now silently landed on the ground below.

"Wow..." Mark marveled, awestruck.

Chastity giggled.

"I told you she was gorgeous!"

———

NOT LONG AFTER, TODD HAD LOST HIS remaining clothes as well. The night-time air was getting chilly, so they'd moved over to the hot tub.

Mark sat next to Jenny, resting his arm on her shoulders. It was an unfamiliar sensation, the feel of another man's body against hers.

The warm water only added to the sensual atmosphere, while the bubbles coming from the seat below gently reminded her of her heightened state of arousal.

Chastity and Todd were getting rather comfortable as well on their side of the tub. She'd taken the lead, tracing her fingertips across his chest while whispering in his ear.

It only took a few moments for her hands to work their way lower.

"Should we swap keys?" Jenny asked, eager to have a good hard cock in her pussy again.

"If you insist," Chastity teased.

They each removed their necklaces and handed them to the other, while Todd and Mark sat up on the edge of the tub to give them unrestricted access.

Jenny looked at Todd, wanting to make sure this was okay. He nodded back.

Turning to face her partner, she rose out of the water to kiss Mark.

Their lips met for a long, passionate moment, and Jenny could feel his cock pressing against the confines of its metal cage.

She slowly kissed her way down his chest and torso until her tongue was teasing his tip through the openings in the cage. The taste of his pre-cum sent her heart racing once again as her lust took over.

"Do you want to fuck me?" she asked Mark.

The question caught her off guard. She wasn't the kind of slut who'd talk to someone else's husband like that, was she? She supposed she was.

A quick glance over at Todd and Chastity revealed they were unfazed by her boldness, if they'd even heard her question at all. They were a little busy at the moment!

"I really want to fuck you," Mark whispered in her ear, making eye contact as she looked up at him before sliding the key into the lock.

CLINK.

With a twist, Mark's cage unlocked and his cock soon sprung to life before Jenny's eyes.

She giggled, running her tongue up and down his length before taking it into her mouth.

"Oh god yes," Mark groaned, gripping the edge of the tub as his cock pulsed in Jenny's mouth.

She let her mouth slide up and down his shaft, enjoying the feeling of his body against hers as he moved his hips.

Then Mark tapped her on the shoulder, pulling her out of the moment. Jenny followed his gaze over to Chastity and Todd, whose cock was still securely locked in its impenetrable steel cage.

Fuck!

"I'm sorry, babe," Jenny said.

"It's okay," Todd said. "Keep doing what you're doing. We like watching!"

"Fuck, yes!" Chastity agreed.

Jenny blushed.

"Okay, then!"

She turned back to Mark, resuming her efforts.

"Oh, fuck..." Todd moaned, clearly enjoying the erotic spectacle of his wife sucking on another man's cock.

It wasn't long before Todd and Chastity had made their way over.

Chastity joined in, giving Jenny a hands-on — or rather tongues-on — demonstration in how to give a double blowjob.

Meanwhile, Todd found his way behind Jenny and was pressing the cold steel cage against her ass while reaching around to finger her clit.

"Oh fuck, baby," Jenny moaned. "That's so good!"

"That's it, Todd," Chastity encouraged. "Make her cum!"

Todd doubled down on her clit, and within seconds Jenny was on the brink of orgasm.

"Yes, yes!" she moaned. "FUCK!"

Her legs wrapped around him as he continued his unrelenting assault until she was trembling with the aftershocks of a powerful orgasm.

"Fuck, you two are hot!" Mark groaned.

Jenny sat back in Todd's lap, content to watch Mark and Chastity do their thing.

"Um, Tiff..." he said, waiting a second for her to pull off of him and make eye contact. "I really want to fuck you. If that's okay with you guys..."

"Please do!" Todd responded eagerly.

Mark hopped back into the water, taking hold of his wife's hands and leading her to the middle of the tub.

He stood up, his erection just rising above the steamy water, and guided her onto him.

Chastity wrapped her legs around him, holding herself in place as she floated on her back in the tub while he fucked her.

It was an incredible sight, and Jenny couldn't help but wish that she was in her position.

But that wasn't in the cards tonight.

"Oh Fuck!" Mark groaned. "YES!"

Mark gave a few more deep thrusts while Chastity's own moans pierced the quiet night.

Once they had finished, Mark sat back down by Jenny while Chastity moved over to Todd, resting her hands on his knees while she floated in the tub.

"I have an idea," Chastity declared with a wild look in her eyes. "Todd, do you want to cum?"

He looked over at Jenny for affirmation.

"Chastity," she smiled, "of course he wants to cum!"

Without a word, Chastity stood up in the water. Her wet, naked body glistened in the moonlight. She was breathtaking.

She reached over to the side of the tub, turning a dial that made the jets come to life.

Jenny leaned back against the chair, enjoying the sensation of the jets pounding away at her back. That's when she got it — Chastity's naughty idea.

"You are brilliant, Chas!" she exclaimed.

"Fuck yes, she is," Todd agreed between gasps of pleasure as Chastity helped him into position with his caged cock inches from one of the powerful jets.

She stood behind him, holding him in place as her once-in-a-generation breasts pressed against the back of Todd's neck.

Jenny wasn't honestly sure if he'd even noticed that, since he seemed entirely preoccupied with whatever the jet was doing for him.

"Oh fuck! Yes!" he moaned. "FUCK!"

Todd's body shook as he came below the water, the jet mercilessly pounding him as Chastity held him firmly in place.

"Fuck! Okay, okay... FUCK!"

Finally Chastity let up, helping him back onto the seat and taking her place by his side.

Todd smiled, then leaned over to give Jenny a deep kiss.

It wasn't the climax she'd been hoping for, but it had been something special.

———

"THANKS AGAIN!" JENNY SAID AFTER THEY'D finished what must have been their fifth goodbye kiss.

"Of course!" Chastity replied. "We can't wait to see you again!"

Jenny was so horny she hadn't even bothered drying off. Her damp dress clung to her body on the drive home, her perky nipples poking through the thin fabric and clearly making it difficult for Todd to keep his eyes on the road!

As soon as they were inside the house, the clothes came off and their bodies met in a fiery kiss.

Todd pushed Jenny up against the wall, holding her hands at our sides as he dropped to his knees and ate her out until she'd had at least one orgasm, maybe more.

By the time they'd made it up the stairs to the bedroom, they were both thoroughly fucked and ready for bed.

"So who's next?" Todd asked.

Jenny laughed.

"Jasmine. She's fun, you'll like her."

"Well, so far, I like all of your friends."

"Mmhmm," she agreed. "So do I! Does that make me a little slut?"

"Absolutely," Todd teased. "But you're my little slut. And I love you just like

77

that."

With that, she snuggled in next to her lover.

Jenny loved being his little slut.

JENNY AND THE CUCKQUEEN COUPLE

PLAYING WITH HER FRIEND'S HUBBY

"HERE WE GO," TODD SIGHED. "LET'S JUST hope third time's the charm!"

"Fourth," Jenny replied softly, enamored with the way the sunlight shimmered through the trees as they drove.

"Huh?"

"Fourth time," she reminded him. "Vanessa was the first."

"Oh! Right."

Since the key party, they'd met up with Vanessa and two other couples already. But the chastity cage wrapped tightly around her husband's package was still securely locked.

Three down, one more to go.

Not that she was complaining, of course. But Jenny desperately wanted his hard cock inside of her again, and the wait was testing her patience.

"I think this is it?" Todd asked rhetorically.

The big blue house in front of them, in a quiet neighborhood on the outskirts of the city, was the last place Jenny would have imagined Jasmine lived.

But if there was one thing she'd learned, it was that this 'lifestyle' was full of surprises.

———

"HELLO, THERE."

The man's deep voice had startled Jenny, his muscular figure towering over her and Todd by a good margin.

It somehow hadn't even occurred to her that Jasmine might have a partner!

"Hi!" Todd answered. "I'm Todd."

He reached out to receive a firm handshake.

"And I'm Jenny!"

"Pleasure to meet you, Jenny," he said in that sultry voice. "I'm Terrance, but you can call me Terry."

84

Terry took her willing hand in his, raising it to his lips for a firm kiss.

Jenny blushed. This guy was damn hot, that was for sure!

"Uh, is Jasmine here?" she asked, wanting to make sure they hadn't come to the wrong house.

"Of course," he assured. "Come on in!"

Terry held the door open for Jenny and Todd, ushering them into the comfortable living room inside.

They sat down on the couch with Jenny in between the two guys.

"Jasmine should be down in a minute," Terry explained.

"No worries!" said Todd.

"So..." Terry sighed, "what brings you two out here?"

"Well, um..." Jenny began, her voice trailing off as Terry softly stroked the small of her back.

"Sorry, is that okay?"

"Yes," Jenny blushed.

It was more than okay. Here she was, this once shy, innocent suburban wife, sitting between two attractive men who both clearly had eyes for her.

"We're still looking for the key," Todd said, nodding down at his crotch.

"Of course," Terry laughed. "First time?"

"Yeah," Jenny sighed, thinking back on all the steamy encounters they'd had over the last few days.

Then it hit her.

Jasmine, along with Vanessa, had been the only two in chastity belts that night. So that must mean...

Jenny subtly looked down at Terry's crotch. He had loose, silky pants on, and she could clearly make out the outline of his cock — uncaged, and rather impressive judging by the outline alone!

"Yeah, I don't lock it up anymore," Terry smiled, having clearly caught her lingering gaze.

Clearly, Jenny hadn't been as subtle as she'd imagined.

"Lucky man!" Todd chimed in.

The three of them shared a laugh at her expense.

"And Jasmine?" she asked.

"Jasmine loves the feel of the belt. It turns her on, leaves her begging for it..."

No shit!

She was about two seconds away from begging for it at the moment herself.

"And besides," Terry smiled, stroking her back to emphasize his point. "We can always do anal still."

Jenny's cheeks burned red at the thought. She was so turned on already, and they hadn't even started anything yet!

"What was that about anal?" a sarcastic voice called out from the stairs.

"Jasmine!"

Jenny stood up, giving her new friend a big hug as she walked into the room.

Todd did as well, except he got a little kiss on the lips from her as well.

"Hey!" Jenny protested with a giggle. "That's not fair!"

She took a step towards Jasmine, hoping for a kiss of her own, only for Terry to spin her around in his arms into a deep, fiery kiss.

It surprised her at first, but soon her body was relaxing — surrendering to his touch.

She finally broke off the kiss, only to find Todd and Jasmine staring at the two of them.

But they weren't upset!

"You can keep going, babe," Todd teased.

"We're just enjoying the show here!" Jasmine added.

"Well, okay then!"

Jenny turned back to Terry, their lips meeting again.

Her eyes closed as his thick arms wrapped around her, and before she knew it he had lifted her up and set her down on the couch without breaking their embrace.

Finally, after what seemed a blissful eternity, Terry pulled away for air.

"Fuck, that's hot!" Todd gasped.

Jenny looked over to find her husband sitting beside them, Jasmine practically sitting in his lap with her arms wrapped around his waist.

"Well, you two certainly don't waste any time!" Jenny giggled.

Terry sat down next to her, giving her a brief reprieve.

"What are you guys into?" he asked.

It was a simple question, but one Jenny wasn't sure she quite knew how to answer.

"I guess we're sort of up for trying anything," Todd responded. "At least once. And maybe twice, just in case we did it wrong the first time."

Jasmine laughed that seductive laugh of hers.

"I really like you two!"

"The feeling is mutual," Jenny agreed.

"What did you have in mind?" Todd asked eagerly.

"If you're up for it..." Terry began.

"We're a little kinky," Jasmine chimed in. "Okay, a lot kinky! So..."

"Would you like to see our play room?"

Jenny liked the sound of that.

"Of course we would!" Todd laughed. "Do you even have to ask?"

They followed their new friends down to the basement. It was like leaving the suburban world with its white picket fences behind.

Down here was an entirely different world. One of polished metallic floors, red lighting, and a metric fuck-ton of sex toys and bondage equipment.

"Holy shit!" Todd exclaimed. "Wow."

"What can I say?" Terry laughed. "I'm a passionate guy!"

"And I'm a damn lucky girl," Jasmine added.

"I'll say," Jenny agreed. "You weren't kidding about a lot kinky!"

"Nope! I'll be the first to admit I'm a total cum slut!"

Jasmine winked, seductively wrapping her body around Todd's and stroking her fingers against his crotch.

"Hey," Todd chimed in. "We're all sluts here."

They all laughed at that one — it was undeniably true!

"So, what catches your eye?" Terry asked.

Jenny looked around the room. There was so much that caught her eye that it was hard to pick one thing!

"Is that a Sybian?" Todd asked, pointing towards a large black sex toy that stood alone in one corner.

"Even better..." Terry said proudly, "a MotorBunny."

"Oooh!" Jenny gasped with a little too much enthusiasm.

She'd heard what they were capable of and had watched some...er...demonstration videos of the legendary toys in use.

"I knew it!" Jasmine squealed. "I knew you were a kinky little slut!"

Jenny shrugged, blushing for the countless time. There was no sense in denying it!

"I'm not sure I'd know how to..." she tried to walk it back.

"Oh, girl! We'll take great care of you, promise!"

"Okay, I guess. What the hell!"

They moved to the corner of the room, the ladies kindly helping each other out of their already minimal attire while Terry plugged the machine in and Todd stood back to admire the view.

"Would you like me to go first?" Jasmine offered.

"Please! But how..." Jenny looked down at the metallic chastity belt tightly wrapped around her friend's waist.

"Oh, I'm used to it." Jasmine said. "In fact, the MotorBunny is perfect for when I'm locked up."

"Really?" Todd asked with great interest.

"Oh yes," she explained, gesturing towards her crotch. "It's the only toy strong enough to make me cum like this!"

"I have to hide the cord sometimes," Terry joked, "or she'll ride this thing for hours on end."

Jenny's mind raced at the thought — hours of pure orgasmic bliss? Yes, please!

———

"MMMMPPHHH..." JASMINE MOANED IN what must have been her sixth orgasm in as many minutes.

Terry had put a ball gag in her mouth after the first two, and Todd was now at the controls learning how to make her squirm.

He was doing a damn good job of it, too!

Jasmine shook as another orgasm crashed over her, a slow and steady stream of her own cum slowly trickling out from behind her belt.

But Jenny had her mind on other things at the moment.

Terry nestled in behind her, pressing himself up against her naked back and running his fingertips across her chest and stomach.

She moaned softly in response, pressing her ass against the growing bulge in his pants.

He was big; that she was pretty sure of. And she really wanted him; that she was very much sure of!

Terry slowly ran his fingers down to her pussy, gently parting her lips as he slipped a finger deep inside and circled her clit with his thumb.

"Oh, God," she gasped as he slowly thrust in and out, in and out.

"You like that, baby?" he whispered in her ear.

"Mmmhmm."

"Good girl."

Todd looked back at her and smiled, shifting so he could watch Jasmine and her at the same time.

Jenny leaned back further into Terry's embrace, his other hand now rising to her breasts to tease her nipples.

"Oh, fuck..." she sighed, her pleasure building with the slow, rhythmic thrusts of his fingers. "I'm gonna..."

"Cum for me, baby," Terry commanded.

"Yes! Yes!" Jenny moaned. "Oh FUCK! FUCK!"

As her orgasm radiated throughout her body, Terry increased his speed and stroke, rapidly finger-fucking her tight pussy until she couldn't take it anymore.

"Okay! Okay!" she gasped as he slowly pulled away and helped her trembling body onto a bench nearby.

Jasmine must have reached her limit as well. Todd had removed her gag and was now helping her off the MotorBunny.

"That was so good..." Jenny panted. "You were so good!"

"My pleasure," Terry said, once again taking her hand in his and kissing it softly — as if he hadn't just fucked her senseless with that same hand!

"You ready to go for a ride, girl?" Jasmine asked, her legs trembling as Todd helped her over to a chair.

Jenny thought for a moment, looking between the MotorBunny and the towering man standing in front of her.

"Uh... If it's okay..." she began.

"Yes?" said Terry.

"I really want you to fuck me."

There. She'd admitted it.

Jenny looked over to Todd and Jasmine, mortified that she'd just said those words as her husband and this man's wife looked on.

But there was no judgement in their eyes, only compersion.

"It's absolutely alright, love!" Todd encouraged.

"As long as we get to watch!" added Jasmine.

Jenny looked up at Terry, a smile forming across her lips as he looked back at her with pure lust in his eyes.

She hadn't noticed, but the bench Terry had helped her onto wasn't some ordinary piece of furniture.

"What is this?" Jenny asked innocently as Terry helped her into position on it.

"It's called a tantra chair," Terry explained, "and it's designed for a singular purpose..."

"Fucking!" Jasmine chimed in.

"Jenny," Terry asked, "do you want me to fuck you?"

She looked at Todd once more, and he eagerly nodded his approval.

"Yes, please!"

Terry wasted no time. With one smooth motion, his pants were off and his impressive cock sprung to life before her.

"Oh, my!"

Jenny couldn't help but giggling. He wasn't quite as big as the enormous dildo which had started this entire journey for them, but he wasn't far off either!

"Damn..." Todd gasped.

Terry rolled an oversized condom down the length of his shaft, the latex stretching tight across its girth.

"You sure you're okay with this?" Terry asked one more time.

Todd was beaming, nodding his affirmation.

"Go for it!" he encouraged.

Terry helped Jenny into position with her back against the cool leather of the chair. He spread her legs wide, fully exposing her dripping pussy as he straddled the middle of the bench.

She was so turned on at the sight of Terry's massive erection that she hadn't even bothered to take a full breath before he was pushing himself inside.

The look on his face was pure carnal desire as her tight pussy gripped his fat cock tightly and pulled him deeper still.

"OH GOD!" Jenny grunted, the pain of the initial penetration quickly fading away to be replaced with the intense sensation of being stretched wider than she ever could've imagined possible with a real, live cock.

"You're so tight, baby!" Terry hissed through clenched teeth, leaning down to give her a tender kiss on the lips.

"Mmmhmmm," Jenny moaned incoherently as waves of pleasure built deep within her.

Each deep thrust pushed her body higher against the back of the chair until finally Terry decided he'd had enough of that.

He reached down and brought both of her legs up to rest on his shoulders, pressing her thighs tight against his chest as he thrust deeper and deeper into her. He leaned down and bit one of her nipples gently, causing her to cry out in delight before rolling it between his fingers.

"Oh yes! Yes! Fuck me!" She begged.

"You're such a slutty little girl…" Terry teased, slowly withdrawing his cock from her pussy only to push it right back inside her.

"Thank… Thank you…" Jenny whimpered, unable to speak above a whisper as his cock drove all the way into her again.

Terry couldn't resist giving her another nibble on the other breast while he fucked her, not to mention several kisses along her neck.

"Yes, baby," he growled. "Give your daddy what he needs."

"That's right!" Jasmine teased. "Fuck that little slut!"

Jenny looked over at Todd. He seemed mesmerized by the scene playing out before him, grinning from ear to ear.

"Terry, fuck my wife!" he commanded. "Fuck her good!"

"As you wish," Terry growled, fucking her even harder and faster than before.

Jenny felt a tingle building insider her. That tingling soon turned into a throb, then a pulse, and finally a full-blown orgasm crashing over her.

She came harder than she ever had with the dildo. Her hips bucked violently against Terry's chest, sending shockwaves of pleasure throughout her body with each spasm.

Jenny's eyes rolled back in her head as the sensation rippled through her; wave after wave as Terry relentlessly fucked her with that incredible cock. She clawed at his back, wanting to pull him inside her deeper still as he continued to pound away.

"Yes! That's it!" Terry moaned.

He slid back on the chair, rotating Jenny's quivering body onto her side without pulling out.

In this position, he could thrust even deeper still while Jenny couldn't help but look her husband and this man's wife in the eyes as she rode his monster cock towards another building orgasm.

"Fuck... fuck..." Jenny whimpered softly. "I'm gonna cum again..."

"Yes!" Terry growled, grinding his thigh against her pussy. "You're such a hot little slut..."

"Oh, God! FUCK!" Jenny cried out as another powerful climax crashed over her like a tidal wave.

She looked over at Todd and Jasmine, a big smile on each of their faces.

"Mmmm, fuck..." Terry groaned as his own orgasm came.

She could feel his cock swell inside her, pulsing as he shot load after load.

Finally, Terry slowly eased the fat tip of his cock out as Jenny collapsed back into the chair, completely spent.

"Fuck, girl, you were amazing!" Jasmine cried, racing over to steal a fiery kiss from her.

"You can say that again!" Todd whispered in Jenny's ear, drawing her in for a kiss of his own.

"Now, your turn?" Jenny asked the two of them.

"Um... not quite," Jasmine hesitated. "I'm a bit of a cuckqueen."

"A what?"

"Cuckqueen," Todd repeated.

"That means I like to watch my man with other ladies," Jasmine explained, "but I don't play with other guys."

Jenny looked up at Todd. She wasn't sure if he'd known that beforehand, but he just shrugged and smiled.

"Fine by me! I can't get enough of watching you either, Jen!"

"Well, whatever floats your boat!" she said. That was the first thing that came to mind! "Should we swap keys, though?"

"Yes, of course," Jasmine replied, starting to remove the key from around her neck.

"No, wait!" Jenny interrupted. "I've got an idea..."

She helped Jasmine onto the chair with her, both of them straddling it as they faced each other.

Then Jenny seductively bent down until her face was practically touching Jasmine's pussy, inserting the key and twisting it until the lock clicked open.

Jasmine slid the cage off, leaving her beautiful and soaked pussy at Jenny's mercy.

"Fuck yes..." Terry moaned, sliding in behind his wife and pinning her arms back to give Jenny unrestricted access.

She ran a finger up and down Jasmine's wet slit, making her shudder and buck at the touch as waves of pleasure coursed through her.

"You're so beautiful, girl," Jenny said, smiling up at her new friend.

It didn't take long before she, with a little help from Terry, had Jasmine squirting all over her and the chair as a long-overdue orgasm rocked her tight body.

"Yes, yes! Holy shit, girl!" Jasmine gasped. "Fuck!"

Jasmine, still trembling from the after-shocks of her orgasm, laid back against Terry and rested her eyes.

"Now, honey," Jenny said, turning her attention to Todd, "let's get your cock back where it belongs!"

She took the necklace from Jasmine, reaching down to insert the key that would undoubtedly unlock her husband's chastity cage.

But the key did not fit the lock.

"What the fuck?" Jenny whispered, trying in vain to get the key to go in.

"Oh shit, man!" Terry added. "Ain't that the last one, too?"

"Yep!"

"I'm sure it will be alright, love," Todd reassured. "Maybe we just need to try the other keys again."

"I... I guess..." Jenny said, though she was confident that she'd given each key a good try.

Each key except...

"It has to be Vanessa's!" she gasped. "Shit! Do you think she did this on purpose?"

Todd shrugged. "I don't know!"

Jenny was more than a little suspicious. Vanessa had been the only one who'd insisted on testing her key in Todd's lock herself.

"Fuck! Okay, let's go find that little bitch and get your cock back, babe!"

"Uh... okay!" he replied.

Jenny looked back at their new friends. The woman who'd been such a great tease. And her man, who'd possibly just given Jenny one of the greatest fuckings of her entire life.

"Thank you both!" she said with a smile.

"What did I tell you, girl?" Jasmine said without so much as opening her eyes. "The pleasure would be all ours!"

"Oh, I remember," Jenny laughed. "But I would have to disagree with that statement!"

"As would I," added Todd.

"Y'all are welcome anytime!" Terry said enthusiastically.

"Well..." Jenny said as naughty thoughts raced through her mind. "We'll swing by sometime!"

That she was absolutely sure of.

JENNY AND THE SWINGERS' CLUB

FIVE HOT GUYS IN ONE HOT NIGHT

"WHAT?"

Jenny could barely make out her friend's voice above the pounding bass.

"Five," Vanessa repeated, raising her hand to emphasize the point.

Her tight body pressed against Jenny's as she leaned in.

"If you want to walk away with that key," Vanessa whispered in her ear, "you're going to have to fuck five different guys tonight."

Vanessa held all the cards, and she damn well knew it.

Jenny had been burning with lust for days — her husband's cock securely locked in the steel chastity cage to which Vanessa held the only key.

"What the fuck, Vanessa?" Jenny seethed, her anger boiling over as she pulled away from her embrace.

Vanessa just stood there looking sexy as fuck, a mischievous grin forming on her lips.

"We'll do it."

Her husband's words were commanding and definitive. Jenny gulped, furious that Todd had just agreed to the demand. There'd be no taking it back now.

"Todd, what the hell..." she began, but he cut her off.

"Come on, Jen," he said, placing his hand on the small of her back and leading her away from Vanessa into the crowd.

The club was packed with at least a hundred swingers, each looking to make the night one to remember.

Todd led her to the crowded dance floor, their bodies bumping up against others as they ground against each other.

She could smell Todd's cologne, his scent intoxicating her with desire. The EDM music was loud, the strong vibrations making her pussy pulse with each beat.

His hands wrapped around her, pulling her closer.

"Jenny," he said in her ear, "I don't want you to do this for Vanessa."

She spun around, pausing for a moment as she searched his expressions. He looked down at her with pure love, his smile making the world stand still for a moment.

"I want you to do this for me."

His words sent a chill down her spine.

"Todd... I... I love you."

"I love you too," he grinned, "my naughty little slut."

Ever since they'd began this journey, she'd been terrified of what her husband might think of her if she really went for it.

But all at once, those fears were gone.

Because Jenny realized, in that moment, that this was what he'd wanted for her all along.

She felt herself responding to him, her heart racing as she took hold of his hands and leaned in for a kiss.

"Mind if I cut in?"

The voice sounded vaguely familiar, but her mind hardly caught up before Todd was handing her off to another mysterious man.

He pressed up against her, just like Todd had been, but the sensation was so different. She could already feel his growing erection pressing against her ass. There was no love in this embrace, only lust — lust for her.

"You look stunning tonight," he said.

Jenny recognized the voice this time, turning around to find Mark.

"Why thank you," she smiled.

At Todd's insistence, Jenny had worn a short silver skirt — with nothing underneath of course — and a sparkling black bra that accentuated her ample breasts. It wasn't an outfit she could wear anywhere else. But here, it was absolutely perfect for the occasion.

"I was hoping we'd run into you tonight," Mark said. "I'd love to pick up where we left off..."

Jenny blushed. They'd left off in the middle of an unfinished blowjob, switching back to each other's partners once they'd realized Todd wouldn't be able to partake that night.

She looked around for a moment, catching a glimpse of her husband. He was a few feet away, dancing with Mark's wife, Chastity.

"We could do that," Jenny teased, "or you could fuck me. Your choice."

She may have given him the choice, but her tone made it clear which she preferred.

"Yes, ma'am! Should we find ourselves a playroom?"

"Um... I guess so!"

Mark tapped on Chastity's shoulder, and soon the four of them had found a small room just off of the dance floor. A soft blue glow illuminated the king-sized mattress, which took up almost the entire room.

"This will do!" Todd said, practically on the edge of his seat with excitement.

They locked the door, and soon were all laying down on the mattress with Jenny in the middle.

Mark crawled on top of Jenny, his erection pressing against her stomach. He stroked his cock as Jenny watched, seductively rolling a condom down the length of his shaft.

Her pussy was throbbing with anticipation, and Mark didn't even bother taking her skirt off. There was no need.

Todd and Chastity had nestled in on either side of her, and were more than happy to help spread her legs as Mark slid the tip of his shaft inside.

"Oh, fuck!" Jenny moaned.

"You are so fucking wet!" Mark gasped in amazement, the realization only making him harder as he pushed deep into her.

Soon enough, his balls slapped against her ass as he fucked her with long, deep strokes. His hands roamed all over her body, stroking her neck and massaging her inner thighs.

Todd and Chastity worked together, licking and sucking both of her nipples in sync with Mark's thrusts.

"Fuck! FUCK!"

It didn't take long for Jenny to cum. Her pussy clamped down hard on Mark's dick, sending him over the edge seconds later.

"Yes, oh fuck!" he grunted, his cock pulsing as spurt after spurt filled the condom.

They all laid there for a while after that, catching their breath as they recovered from the intense orgasms.

———

A FEW MINUTES LATER, THEY WERE SAYING goodbye and heading back out to the dance floor.

"One down," Todd said. "Four to go."

Jenny nodded. She felt so naughty, already on the hunt for her next score with her own juices still dripping down her thighs from having just been fucked by Mark.

The dance floor was a little less crowded as couples paired off and headed for the playrooms, and it didn't take long before they ran into some more friends with whom they had unfinished business.

Tiffany and Nathan were lifestyle newbies as well, and seemed reluctant to initiate. But Todd had her back, and after a few minutes of small talk, he stepped in to get things going.

"Nate, Tiff," he said in the polished tone of a true salesperson, "would you two like to fuck my wife now?"

They exchanged nervous glances before looking back at Jenny and Todd with big smiles on their faces.

"That would be an enthusiastic yes!" Tiffany giggled.

By now, most of the playrooms were occupied. Fortunately, they walked over just as another group was walking out and jumped at the opportunity.

They stepped inside and locked the door, their eyes adjusting to seductive red mood lighting and maroon-painted walls.

This, it seemed, was the BDSM room they'd heard others talk about.

"Wow!" Nathan said.

"What would you like, honey?" Todd said, his voice dripping with sexual undertones.

Jenny looked around, taking in all the options.

There was a Sybian, a queen sized bed with mounting points for restraints, and a St. Andrew's cross in one corner of the room.

"Um..." she began, holding back a bit.

"Don't be shy," Todd encouraged. "Ask for what you want, love!"

She smiled at her husband, then turned to the other couple.

"I'd really love to try the cross, if you don't mind."

"Oh, we certainly don't mind!" Tiffany giggled. She was having way too much fun with this!

They might have been newbies, but it didn't take long before the three of them had Jenny blindfolded and secured to the four corners of the cross.

Her legs were spread wide, and she could feel the cool air on her slick pussy. It made her even more horny for what was to come next.

There was a brush of leather against skin, and Jenny gasped in anticipation.

"Shhh," Todd commanded, giving her a nice smack on the ass with one of the floggers.

"Oh, fuck!"

"That's right, oh fuck," he teased, giving her a second firm whack.

That one stung a bit!

"Let me help," Tiffany offered.

She gently brushed a fleece cloth over Jenny's skin, soothing the sting. It was so soft, a tantalizing contrast to the harsh leather.

Todd and Tiffany continued their game of cat-and-mouse, stingy-and-soft for a few minutes, driving Jenny absolutely wild.

She thrashed against the cuffs binding her wrists and ankles, but it was no use.

"You okay, love?" Todd asked.

"Yeah," Jenny panted. "But I'm so fucking horny!"

"Would you like me to fuck you?" Nathan asked.

His offer was a welcomed relief from the agonizing anticipation that had been building for the past few minutes.

"Yes."

No more words were spoken.

Nathan stepped up behind her, sliding a condom on before slipping his hard cock in.

"Ohhhh!"

"Good girl," Nathan whispered, slowly building up his speed.

Todd stood beside her, tracing the flogger up and down her side as Nathan fucked her harder and harder.

She moaned out loud with each thrust.

Being bound to the cross and unable to move or see what was happening was a turn on like nothing she'd ever experienced before.

"Fuuuuck!" she moaned, gripping the bars of the cross as Nathan pounded away at her.

"Do you want to cum, Jenny?" Tiffany teased.

"Yes!"

Nathan pulled out, leaving her desperate for release. Her pussy trembled, juices dripping onto the floor below as she begged for me.

"Please!," Jenny cried. "Fuck me!"

He stepped forward again, and with one deep thrust he was balls deep in her pussy.

"FUCK!"

Her orgasm was quick and strong, accompanied by moans that echoed throughout the playroom.

But Nathan wasn't done with her yet, thrusting faster and faster in pursuit of his own release.

"Oh fuck, I'm gonna cum!" he warned.

He erupted inside her, sending Jenny over the edge a second time.

When he finally pulled out, Jenny was left shaking with the aftershocks.

Todd and Tiffany helped her off of the cross, giving her and Nathan a moment to recover on the bed after their adventure.

Jenny laid back on the cool sheets, feeling as if she could snuggle up and fall asleep right here. But then she saw Todd discretely hold up a hand with four fingers, pulling his pinky in with his thumb to leave three.

Fuck, this was going to be a long night!

———

ONCE AGAIN, THEY THANKED THEIR PLAY partners and parted ways.

Jenny and Todd headed back to the dance floor, but found most of the crowd had dissipated by now. But judging by the near-continuous stream of moans from the various playrooms, the night was still young.

"Hey you two!" Vanessa squealed with excitement, making a beeline for them.

Jenny wasn't sure she wanted to talk to her just now, but Todd waved her over regardless.

"How's it going?" Vanessa inquired.

"Two down," Todd smiled. "Three more to go."

"Damn, Jenny! You better hurry it up a bit!"

She rolled her eyes at the two of them, who were clearly enjoying her predicament.

"Vanessa," Todd asked, "do you have any ideas for how we might... speed things up a bit?"

A mischievous look flashed across her face.

"Do I ever..." Vanessa purred, taking Jenny's reluctant hand and guiding her across the floor.

Jenny looked back, realizing that Todd wasn't following along for the moment. She hesitated, but he gave her a smile and a wave for reassurance.

She followed Vanessa around the corner into a small, dark booth.

"What is this?" Jenny asked, fearing she already knew the answer.

"You still want that key back, Jen?"

"Fuck! Of course I do!"

"Then welcome to the glory hole..."

Vanessa's words, delivered with a flair for dramatic effect, sent Jenny's pulse racing as she followed her friend's eyes to a circular cutout in the wall.

"You ready?"

"Um... I guess so."

"Good."

Taking a step over towards the wall, Vanessa flicked a switch that lit up the room in a deep purple glow.

That must have been the signal they were open for business, for not five seconds later there was a fully-erect penis poking through and waiting to be serviced.

"On your knees..." Vanessa instructed, guiding Jenny into position in front of the unfamiliar cock.

Though she couldn't be certain, Jenny guessed that the man on the other side was older than anyone she'd played with so far. That thought seemed both a little creepy and a little arousing at the same time.

"He's waiting!" Vanessa reminded, putting a hand on Jenny's neck to help move her along.

Her mouth opened instinctively, taking this complete stranger's shaft into her lips. He was decently well-endowed, and she could taste the tang of his pre-cum as it slid down her throat.

She swirled her tongue around the tip before taking him in deep as Vanessa guided her up and down the length of his shaft.

"Mmmm," he groaned, bucking softly and almost making her gag.

She took her time, savoring the feel of his member as it filled her mouth, stroking him slowly as she worked her way down to the base and back again.

After a minute of this, she got down to business.

"Come on, slut," Vanessa cooed.

Jenny bobbed her head faster and faster, feeling his quickening pulse against the roof of her mouth.

"That's it," Vanessa whispered. "Harder."

She complied, pushing herself further and faster than she'd ever gone before.

"Oh, fuck..." came a groan from the other side, followed by three taps on the wall.

Jenny guessed what that meant.

"Keep going," Vanessa commanded.

"Mmmphhh," Jenny tried to reply, but her lips were occupied.

"It doesn't count if you don't finish him off..."

Fuck! Vanessa could be so persuasive when she set her mind to it.

Jenny looked ahead, swirling her tongue from side to side as she slid all the way forward until his tip was nearly touching the back of her throat.

"FUCK!"

The man's cock swelled before unleashing several quick spurts of cum into Jenny's throat.

She swallowed quickly, trying to take it all, but some splashed out onto her chest as he bucked against her for another few seconds.

Finally, he pulled back. Jenny peered through the hole, but couldn't make out any details of the complete stranger she'd just deep-throated.

Holy shit, she had actually done that!

"Excellent work," Vanessa purred, turning Jenny's face towards hers and embracing.

Their lips met in a sensual kiss.

For all the anger she'd felt towards Vanessa the past few days, she couldn't deny the appreciation she had for this woman who'd opened up her world in such a profound way.

"Oh, shit!" Vanessa exclaimed, pulling back to look at her watch.

"What?"

"It's 1:30 already," Vanessa said with mock-horror.

Oh shit, indeed! The club would only be open for another thirty minutes, and Jenny still needed to fuck two more guys if they were going to get that key back tonight.

———

"LET'S GO!"

Jenny stood up, racing out of the booth towards the main dance floor, when a familiar voice stopped her in her tracks.

"Hey girl!" Jasmine squealed as she ran towards them. "Oh my, what have we here?"

In her rush to get back out there, Jenny had forgotten to clean up the stranger's cum, which was still dripping from her lips.

"Damn it!" Jenny gasped, attempting to cover up her complete sluttiness.

"It's okay, girl!" Jasmine reassured. "We're all sluts here!"

Jenny looked around the room. Half the people standing around were partially or fully naked, undoubtedly having just come from the playrooms without so much as bothering to put their clothes back on.

"I guess you're right," Jenny said, smiling at the realization.

"Pardon me," Vanessa interrupted, "but you've only got twenty-five minutes and two cocks to please!"

Jenny blushed, while Jasmine laughed out loud.

"Yes, your husband was telling us!" she said.

"Us?" Jenny asked.

"Yes, us," Jasmine teased, pointing across the room. "Terry's with your man."

The mention of Jasmine's husband instantly sent her libido into overdrive. Terry was not only incredibly sexy, he was incredible in bed as well.

"Do you think..." she trailed off.

"Yes, I think he would love to fuck you, girl!"

Jasmine held nothing back. That was for sure.

"Well, what are we waiting for?" Vanessa laughed.

The three women crossed the room together, drawing lustful glances from most of the men and a good number of the women in the club.

Terry and Todd stood up as they approached, both of them mesmerized by Jenny.

"Damn," Terry finally said. "You are a lucky man."

"Damn right I am," Todd responded.

Vanessa took a step forward.

"This girl," she said in a voice loud enough for more than the five of them to hear, "needs two hard cocks in the next twenty-five minutes!"

"Shhh, Vanessa!" Jenny scolded her, to no avail.

"Well, I'd be more than happy to help," Terry said in his deep, sexy voice.

Before Jenny's mind had caught up with her body, they were passionately kissing. Terry picked her up and walked her over to the couch, setting her down gently without so much as breaking the kiss.

He finally paused to catch his breath, unbuttoning his shirt and tossing it to the floor.

Jenny was speechless for a second, admiring the ripped man in front of her who, for some crazy reason, seemed to want her as much as she wanted him.

"Uh... should we go to a playroom?" Jenny asked.

Terry shook his head.

"No time," Todd chimed in.

"I'm okay right here, baby," Terry whispered. "If you are."

"I'm okay!" Jenny could hardly believe the words had come out of her mouth. But she'd meant them.

Here she was, racing to fuck five guys in one night at a swingers' club. Did it really make a difference whether it was in a private room or out here in the open? She thought not.

Terry's lips met hers again, and soon the others were joining them on the couch.

Todd helped Jenny out of her skirt, while Jasmine put a condom on her husband's incredible cock.

Jenny suddenly became very aware of the wetness building between her legs.

It probably helped that Vanessa was gently stroking her pussy, something she hadn't even realized at first with all the sensory overload.

Terry's hand joined Vanessa's, his thick fingers probing Jenny's pussy and curling into a hook to stimulate her g-spot.

"That feels so good," she moaned, surrendering to her desire.

She heard a snap, opening her eyes to see Jasmine liberally applying lube to Terry's shaft.

"Jazz, I think I'm wet enough already," Jenny gasped between moans.

"Not for this, you aren't…" Terry teased, effortlessly lifting her onto his lap as his thick cock slid deep into her asshole.

"Oh, God!" she panted as he stretched her tight little hole.

Jasmine gave her a playful slap on the ass, while Vanessa got straight to work stroking her clit.

"Yes! Yes!" Jenny repeated in a half-delirious state of pure sexual bliss.

She threw her head back against Terry's shoulder, arching her back as he rhythmically pounded her.

He thrusted deep into her, working her over relentlessly.

"You like my big cock, slut?" he growled in her ear.

"I fucking love it!" Jenny replied, knowing that was exactly what he was hoping to hear.

As if reading her mind, he began pounding her even harder than ever before.

"That's a good girl," he whispered in her ear.

That was enough to send her crashing over the edge, a huge orgasm rushing through her body as she moaned Terry's name.

"Hey, I can't let you two have all the fun," Todd whispered in her ear.

Jenny opened her eyes again, following her husband's gaze down to his now unlocked and fully erect cock!

She looked back up as he smiled at her, and Jenny knew exactly what he had in mind.

"Yes," she moaned.

Todd dropped to his knees, sliding his own cock into her pussy as Terry continued to pump her asshole from behind.

She'd been double penetrated by a dildo before, but this was a whole different experience.

"Fuck!" she whimpered as Todd's cock pushed deeper inside her.

"That's it, Jenny," he smiled. "Take us both!"

She did, moaning as these two incredible men fucked her hard.

Terry might have been an incredible lover on his own, but he was no match for the two of them together.

"So... fucking... good..." she panted.

She could feel the orgasm rising in her, and it was even deeper and stronger than anything she'd experienced before.

"Oh God... FUCK!" Jenny said, unleashing a primal scream as the massive wave of pleasure rippled through her.

That seemed to be all it took for Terry and Todd, who came at almost the exact same time.

When they finally slowed to a stop, Jenny simply laid there between the two of them, well fucked and completely spent.

Todd slid his cock out first, unleashing a flood of warm cum which ran down her legs and pooled on the floor.

Then Terry took her by the waist, gently helping her off of him.

She sat between Terry and Todd, catching her breath as she finally noticed the crowd that had gathered around them to watch the show.

Some of them were now pleasuring each other, and at least one older man was rapidly pumping his dick while staring her down.

That was both super awkward and super hot!

"So, the key?" Jenny finally said after a few minutes.

Vanessa shrugged.

"Ask your husband."

She looked over at Todd, confused. He grinned, holding it up for her to see.

"I've got a confession to make," he said. "I had the key the whole time."

"What?!" Jenny gasped. "But why?"

He smiled back at her with that same look of pure love that never seemed to fade.

"Because I wanted you to do this," he explained, motioning towards the friends gathered around them.

Friends they'd had the great pleasure of playing with in their search for the key that Todd had apparently had all along.

"Not for me," he said with a smile, "but for you."

FROM THE AUTHOR

Thank you for checking out
***The Jenny Collection
Series Two***

It's hard for books to get
noticed these days. Whether
you liked this one or not, please
consider writing a review.

Thanks so much!
Christian Price

———

CHRISTIANPRICEWRITES.COM

ALSO BY CHRISTIAN PRICE

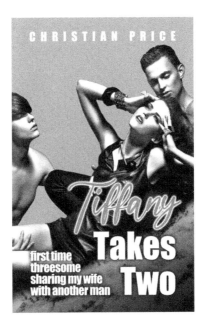

**Tiffany wants the undivided attention
of *two* sexy men at the same time.** But
when things don't go quite to plan, will she
surrender to her desires and let the intense
passion of the moment get the best of her
while her husband watches?

.

Printed in Great Britain
by Amazon

26468819R00088